Praise for *Scent of a White Rose*

"...everything about Scent of a White Rose was such a fresh new concept when it came to vampires, actually it was just a whole new concept in general for the paranormal genre! This is a read any paranormal lover should read!" ~ YA-Aholic

"Thawer managed what I thought was an impossible feat. She was able to put yet another new spin on the age old vampire tale." ~ The Bookshelf Sophisticate

"The highly imaginative plotline is full of kick-ass twists and builds up in intensity the further you get into the book. The concept of "drifting" in which the feelings of vampires are visible through the changing colors of their hair, eyes and skin at different stages of their emotions, tickled me pink and fascinated me. Everything comes nicely together by the end of the story, with enough left over for the next book in the series." ~ Books 4 Tomorrow

Praise for *Roses & Thorns*

"If you're a romantic at heart you'll love this forbidden vampire romance filled with emotion and enchanting characters. Roses & Thorns is the perfect follow up to the first book in the Rose Trilogy..." ~ Romancing the Darkside

"I have lost count of all the things I love about this short story. The imagery she used to describe the tender relationship between Rose and her mother Loraine is breathtaking. It is truly heartwarming and will leave you wanting more." ~ The Booklovers Realm

"Totally loved this book! Loved the way the story just flowed. The characters are so loveable. Christian the vampire, is just dreamy.....swoon worthy even. The way he is so kind and caring towards the humans and toward Rose made you just melt at his every word." ~ Brenda, Goodreads Reviewer

Praise for *Blood of a Red Rose*

"The whole idea of, What do you do if by being with the love of your life, you could throw them into madness and eternal darkness? is just fascinating. And, of course, this easily five-of-five-star read executed the concept beautifully." ~ Ricochet Reviews

"WOW! This book was even better than the first book in the series! Tish Thawer is an amazing author, and after reading book one and two of her Rose Trilogy, I am officially hooked and obsessed! This is a series you do not want to miss!" ~ YA-Aholic

"Just when you think you know where the story of Rose and Christian is going, author Tish Thawer adds several twists and turns to the storyline for book two of the Rose Trilogy. Actually, I love when an author puts in surprises which takes the reader to a place they hadn't even considered..." ~ DiAnn, Goodreads Reviewer

Praise for *Aradia Awakens*

"I was amazed by the sentence fluidity and how fast I read this one. I wanted more: after each sequence that included Aryiah and Damarius, I was ecstatic! Tish knows how to get a grip on me with all those delicious scenes!" ~ Proserpine Craving Books

"Ok Tish Thawer, I must thank you for this captivating fantasy world you created in Aradia Awakens! Some hot scenes between the main characters kept me turning the pages for more, as well as colorful dialogue had me laughing out loud! Looking forward to more!!" ~ Book Lovers Realm

"I like Aryiah's character, she was often very confused by all the changes in her life, but she managed those changes well. Her relationship with Damarius is hot, and I felt the chemistry between them. The more Aryiah learned about the other world of Ovialell, the more intriguing the story became for me. The magic and setting are unique. Now that the foundations for the world have been laid, I am looking forward to the next installment in the series." ~ Book Savvy Babe

BEHIND THE VEIL

~ *An Ovialell Series Omnibus* ~

by

Tish Thawer

Amber Leaf Publishing

Divide, Colorado

First Edition; Includes the short-stories:
Prophecy's Child, The Rise of Rae, and Shay and the Box of Nye

Please note: While these short-stories are all YA and appropriate for teens, the main books in the Ovialell series are adult in nature and are NOT intended for readers under the age of 18.

ISBN: 978-0-9891585-4-1
Library of Congress Control Number: 2013905300
Cover design by Regina Wamba of Mae I Design

Amber Leaf Publishing, Divide, Colorado
www.amberleafpublishing.com
www.tishthawer.com

Acknowledgements

Thank you to my wonderful fans. Your demands for these stories to be in print is what inspired me to compile this book. Thank you for your continued support.

Regina Wamba: Thank you for yet another job well done!

And a special thank you to my nephew, Daniel. Your desire to share these stories with your friends and teachers makes me very proud. I love you.

TISH THAWER

PROPHECY'S CHILD

~ AN OVIALELL SERIES COMPANION ~

PROPHECY'S CHILD

by

Tish Thawer

 CHAPTER ONE

Kylie's throat was on fire. She literally couldn't scream anymore. The moment the demons entered her home, she tried to grab her little sister and flee, but she just wasn't fast enough.

"Don't worry about the little one," one of the demons said. "She's too young to enter the breeding program. But you...you'll do just fine." The menace in his voice had Kylie screaming through the pain of her raw vocal cords.

After dragging her outside, the demons threw her into the back of the transport carriage, which was nothing more than a metal cage on the back of an old wooden wagon. Once she righted herself, she took in the faces of the other sobbing women. There was Trina, the blacksmith's daughter, and her cousin Lucy, along with Avetta, the storekeeper's wife, and Reni, the stablemaster's sister.

Kylie kept a cautious eye on the guards as they made their way to the front of the carriage. Once she was sure they were out of earshot, she turned to the women. "Don't be afraid. I'll do everything within my power to get us out of here." The girls looked at her with hope blooming in their eyes, then immediately dried their tears. They knew that if anyone could save them it would be Kylie.

Kylie was twenty-three and had *matured* years ago. With her long dark hair and tall slender figure, she was a perfect candidate for the breeding program. She grew up hearing stories of the evil queen and her red-eyed demons from Abrinthill. They roamed the three realms, gathering female prisoners in order to continue their race, but they'd never set foot in her realm...until now.

Luckily for the women, Kylie wasn't the average prisoner. She had powers that no one else in the village had had for over five-hundred years. Her village sat on an ancient vortex of magick, one that the former spirit women utilized to sustain the prosperity of their land.

It was foretold that once every five-hundred years a new spirit woman would be born in order to continue the magickal workings. When Kylie was born, the priests divined that she would be the village's next spirit woman. Once they verified she bore the mark of the prophecy's child—a crescent moon on the inside of her thigh—they waited until her thirteenth birthday to begin her training as was customary.

The priests didn't possess any magick, but were educated in how to prepare the blessed women for their duties. The old texts that guided them in the ancient ways were kept secret in the catacomb library of the abandoned church. The books' location was passed down from generation to generation.

Once Kylie had been properly trained in the ways of her magick, she ventured to the lowest level of the abandoned church where she bathed in the Spring of Spirits. There, she completed the ritual to seal her powers and become the current prophecy's child.

As Kylie's home was being raided, on the other side of the village, Rezmona entered the church. She expected to hear screams, but instead was met with silence.

"Where's Gregor?" she snapped.

The guards on duty stood at attention. "My Queen. Gregor said to let you know we are in the process of moving the prisoners."

That explained the silence, but not the reason behind it. The deserted church had served as a good base of operations for months now.

"I believe you'll find him in, um...in the office," the other guard stuttered. His eyes found the floor as he shifted nervously on his feet.

Rezmona's stare bore into him for a fraction of a second, then she headed towards the office without giving a response. The guard exhaled a sigh of relief.

The hall, with its moss covered walls and heavy wooden doors, was bathed in flickering candlelight. Rezmona recognized the feelings of homesickness, but quickly shut them down. If they were moving the prisoners, returning home wasn't something that was going to happen anytime soon.

Rezmona was the demon queen of Abrinthill, the largest and most lavish city in all of the realms. She was beautiful, but also the most brutal queen that had ever ruled.

She had long black hair, a shapely figure, plump ruby lips, and blood red eyes. But along with her gothic inspired skirts and corsets, her appearance was only an illusion she cast. A demon's true nature was only revealed when they shed their glamour, which they didn't do often. However, on the rare occasion they did, their true form was that of large, red-skinned towering beasts. They wore no clothes, which left them naked and exposed, and each with a set of horns which protruded from their heads.

When Rezmona claimed her natural form, her horns were stunning. Shiny black with gold stripes running through them, resembling a tiger's eye stone. They curved and spiraled into perfect points, which truly made her a sight to behold in either form. As the queen, she was also the only female demon whose eyes still glowed red and who was allowed to travel outside their city of Abrinthill.

Centuries ago, the females of their race suddenly began to lose the color of their eyes. Panic ensued when it was soon discovered they were no longer able to reproduce. The only explanation the elders offered was that their race was being punished by the Gods for constantly reproducing with world domination being their only goal.

At the time, the only blessing was that the queen's eyes had retained their natural hue. With the help of her mentors, she'd perfected the dark magick needed to continue their race, although at a much slower pace. The breeding program was founded, and ever since, the continuation of their existence solely depended upon impregnating the prisoners they collected from across the three realms.

The last time Rezmona and her demons made one of these gathering trips, they'd gained over sixteen new prisoners–each fertile and ready to enter the breeding program. Although the program was a success, it didn't change the fact that leaving the palace was something she never looked forward to.

When Rezmona entered the church office she found Gregor hunched over the desk reading from a tattered old book. "Gregor, what is the meaning of this? Why are we moving the prisoners?"

He took a moment to mark his place, then looked up at her with tired eyes. "Just a precaution, my Queen. We have stayed here for far too long, and if we plan to collect more prisoners, we had better move now, before their loved ones attempt a rescue."

Easing her way across the room with a serious look on her face, Rezmona suddenly slammed her hands down on the old wooden desk. "That is no reason to move the prisoners! I could crush anyone who attempted such a foolish mission. Now, what's the real reason we are leaving, and what is it that you're reading?"

Gregor, her mentor, had served her mother and grandmother before her. He wore a long hooded robe to conceal his weathered face, because even under his glamour, age had clearly left its mark on this centuries-old demon. He walked with a tall wooden staff, presenting an image of an old and feeble demonic monk. But just as his appearance was an illusion, so was that assumption. Gregor's magick was extremely powerful, and in his prime, he was considered one of the most vile men in Abrinthill.

He squinted slightly, then gathered the book into his robe. "Just an old manuscript regarding the history of the town and its people. I found it here in the church."

Gregor was known to be a history buff so this shouldn't seem out of the ordinary. Seeming to relax ever so slightly, she asked, "Have you learned anything of value from it?"

"Nothing extraordinary. The church was founded over three thousand years ago. The people of the village lived modestly, and their town has always been very prosperous."

Gregor motioned for her to follow him out the door.

"Prosperity is good. Hopefully that will translate to the fertility of their women as well," Rezmona replied, then followed her mentor to the carriage waiting at the back of the church.

"And to answer your previous question, my Queen, the main reason I've decided to move the prisoners has to do with the amount of time we'll be staying. I know how much you hate having to leave Abrinthill, so my plan is to gather enough prisoners this trip to sustain the breeding program for at least a solid year. If that goal is met, we would soon run out of room here in the church," Gregor explained. "I've started moving the prisoners to the abandoned castle on the outskirts of town. Even though the transport from the village will take longer, the castle will serve as a good base of operations until we are ready to return home."

Rezmona remembered the castle he was referring to. She'd noticed it during their initial trip into town. The back of it literally hung over a cliff, and the front was easily defended. He was right...it would serve as a perfect base. As she entered the carriage the idea of not having to leave Abrinthill for over a year put a smile on her face. "Continue dealing with the prisoners, Gregor. I'll meet you at the castle when you're done."

* * * * *

Gregor hadn't heard Rezmona approaching the office, so when she caught him reading from the ancient text, it had indeed startled him. And though her questioning his motives had set his teeth on edge, he quickly diffused the queen's anger with his even-keeled response because he wasn't ready to discuss what he'd found within the manuscript just yet. At present, he was only a quarter way through the book, but due to his powers of foresight knew it was important to finish it as soon as possible.

The day they'd entered the town, he'd been immediately drawn to this church, and after weeks of searching the ruins, he found the tattered book buried deep within its catacomb library. The moment he held it in his hands, he sensed it was

imperative to gain the knowledge within, but the question of

why still remained.

Kylie glanced around the cage then shut her eyes and took a deep breath. But just as she started to draw on her magick, her plan of a break out was thwarted.

A cloaked man was walking towards the back of the carriage, leaning heavily on a cane, or rather a staff, and was mumbling something under his breath.

The moment the man reached the cage, Kylie knew she had missed her opportunity to save the women and escape. After seeing a gray mist drift from the end of his staff, she watched as each of them immediately drifted to sleep. As her eyes started to fall, the last thing Kylie saw was the old man leering down at them with glowing red eyes and a grim smile on his face.

* * * * *

Kylie had been raised in a loving home surrounded by her mother and father, her three older brothers, and her younger sister. Growing up, her parents would tell them stories of the demons from Abrinthill, and from what she could recall, the man who cast the sleeping spell had to have been the queen's mentor; for only he and the queen had the ability to wield such magick.

Kylie woke in a large stone enclosure, and after shaking off the effects of the spell, she quickly looked around to locate the other girls from her village. They were all huddled together, softly sobbing.

"Do you know where we are?" she asked the girls.

They all shook their heads. Kylie moved towards the barred door and looked up and down the corridor. She saw multiple cells containing many other crying women.

"We look to be in a dungeon of some sort. Have there been any signs of guards or that old man again?"

"No," Trina replied. "We only woke a few moments before you and haven't seen anyone."

"Okay. I'm going to go to the back of the cell and prepare to draw on my magick. Please alert me if anyone starts to come this way."

Kylie then moved into the farthest, darkest corner of the cell she could find. Settling down on the floor, she closed her eyes and took a deep breath as she began to ground and center herself. The feeling of the cold stones beneath her fell away as she tapped into the warmth of the earth. Once an invisible protective bubble formed around her, creating a sacred space, Kylie began to chant. "Spirit realm, open to me. Allow this prophecy's child to see. Give me the powers that I need, to protect these women and set us free."

The amount of energy that surged into Kylie's body was more than she'd ever experienced. Like a collision of all the elements flowing into her at once. The heat of a hot southern fire, the caress of a breeze from the east, a cool spray from the oceans of the west, all mixed with the density of an earthbound oak tree from the north. The magick was so powerful, Kylie knew she'd now be able to withstand anything these demons attempted.

Just as she gave thanks to the spirit realm and closed her impromptu circle, Kylie heard footsteps approaching. It seemed the time to put her new magick to the test was quickly approaching.

Once Rezmona settled into her new room within the castle, she started to prepare for the prisoners' inspection.

The queen was the only demon who could harness the dark powers required to make the breeding program a success and therefore traveled with the raiding parties.

It was discovered long ago that a human couldn't successfully carry a demon's child unless dark magick was used. After several unsuccessful attempts and multiple torturous deaths, Rezmona's ancestors finally found the right combination of magick which would allow a demon child to be born successfully through the program.

With her dark magick starting to flow, she followed a guard to the dungeon. She had a good feeling the new prisoners were going to make suitable hosts and was anxious to begin the process.

As they made their way to the dungeon, she took the opportunity to study the castle's decor. For being abandoned, it was still in decent shape. The stone walls were dry and intact, and the candelabras were polished and lit, creating a warm glow throughout.

She wondered if Gregor had used his magick to spruce things up before her arrival. If she was going to be forced to remain away from her home for an extended period, he sure as hell better do everything he could to make her stay tolerable. He knew better than to ignore her basic comforts.

As they rounded the stairs that led to the dungeon, Rezmona felt a slight tingle along her skin which indicated magick had recently been used. She grinned as she assumed Gregor was doing something else to improve their living conditions.

The moment they reached the first cell, she started to chant under her breath. The magick necessary for the breeding program was more difficult to wield than her normal magick, and therefore required incantations. "Fill this demon, darkest of dark, allow me to measure these prisoners' spark."

The black energy flowed across her skin, leaving visible veins of dark magick winding up and around her arms, across her torso, and up her neck until it filled her blood red eyes, causing them to change into pools of black death.

As she stepped up to the first cell door, the women within started to scream. Rezmona smiled maniacally; their screams intensifying the burn of the dark magick as it flowed through her veins. Rezmona raised her hands and started the inspection process.

Her dark magick flowed like tentacles from her hands and wrapped around each of the women one by one. The searing pain it caused was evident by the screams that continued to fill the dungeon. The strands of magick dug into the women's skin, first centering on their wombs to verify their fertility.

If the women were fertile, then the process continued to prepare their bodies for impregnation. Their DNA was altered slightly, and their minds were placed in a drugged state. If the women weren't able to bear children, the tendrils of dark magick centered around their hearts, effectively killing them in order to put them out of their misery.

Rezmona thought that killing the infertile slaves was an amazing feature the elders had worked into the magickal inspections. Because honestly, as a race whose main goal was to populate the world, the idea of being unable to bear children was worse than death. The irony of this wasn't lost on her. Finding a way around their sterility had been the crowning achievement of her race. Their demon culture was smart, strong, and unstoppable, nature be damned.

CHAPTER FIVE

After listening to screams for what seemed like an eternity, Kylie was startled when she was suddenly met with silence. The approaching footsteps had her scrambling to her feet. When a woman with eyes as black as coal appeared outside their cell, Kylie could only assume she was staring at Rezmona, the demon Queen of Abrinthill.

As the queen stepped up to the door, all the women in the cell huddled around Kylie. Just as Rezmona raised her hands, Kylie stepped in front of the small crowd. She didn't know exactly what she needed to do to defend against the queen, but as Kylie raised her arm she hoped the new magick flowing through her would be enough to stand against this evil woman.

"Stop. At least tell us what you're preparing to do to us."

Fury radiated from Rezmona as she waved her hand, causing the barred door to completely disappear. Once inside, the door reappeared back in place.

"How dare you speak to me," she said in a low, menacing tone. "You are a lowly prisoner, a breeding pig, and now you will pay for your impudence."

Rezmona's threat hung in the air as her eyes deepened once more. She raised her hands, and with an evil smirk on her face, stalked towards the women.

The look on Rezmona's face had Kylie preparing for the worst, but when the queen raised her hands...nothing happened. She shook her arms, chanted something under her breath, and then flung her hands in their direction again.

Kylie remained a single soldier standing in front of the scared women. She felt the tingle of magick flow down her outstretched arm and couldn't pinpoint any particular purpose to it, but right now she didn't care. It was obvious the spirit realm had filled her with the exact magick that was needed, and she couldn't have been more grateful.

After letting out a howling scream, Rezmona flew back towards the barred door in a fit of wild rage. The door flew open, pinning one of the guards between it and the cell itself. Kylie watched in horror as Rezmona slammed the door repeatedly against the poor guard's body until he was nothing more than a bloody heap.

Once the queen was gone, the other guards shut the cell door and carried off their dead brother. Only then did Kylie lower her hand. Staring at her palm in shock, she was stunned to see a small blue spiral emblazoned there. Closing her eyes, she chanted her thanks to the spirit realm once more. "Thank you for bestowing me with the specific gifts that I'll need. I'm forever your servant, that's my vow and for this gift, I thank you now." The spiral glowed, tingled, and then settled into a permanent tattoo on Kylie's palm.

The women rushed to Kylie, throwing their arms around her while sobbing their thanks. She didn't feel as if she'd done anything miraculous, but after hearing the screams resonate from the other cells and witnessing the queen's wrath, she knew they truly did have something to be thankful for.

As she gathered the women in prayer, she couldn't help but wonder if her magick was just a one-time thing. She didn't want to think about what would happen to her friends if she wasn't there when they needed protecting. Suddenly, she knew that not only was she there to protect them, but also to fight for them.

With this realization running through her head, Kylie turned to the women. "Have any of you ever used a weapon?"

The women just stared at her, mouths gaping.

"We're going to have to fight in order to get out of here, and I need to know if you're all willing to do that. Because your freedom and your lives depend on it."

The women slowly nodded their heads in agreement. "Good. Now we need to find something I can transform into weapons. We are surrounded by stone, so see if you can find any loose shards or bricks from the walls and bring them to me."

The women fanned out and began running their hands along the walls and floor. Moments later, they had gathered a small pile of rubble in the corner of the cell.

Kylie sent the women to watch the dungeon hall as she gathered her spirit magick into a protective bubble once more.

After welcoming the flowing energy into her again, Kylie placed her hands over the stones and chanted, "Stone from earth, earth from heart, transform these shards into weapons of art."

The pile of rubble was then surrounded with a beautiful green pulsing light. The stones began to shimmer and shake and were then transformed into the most beautiful knives and daggers Kylie had ever seen. They were encrusted with emeralds and sapphires, rubies and citrine–all gifts from the earth.

Kylie knew these magickally enhanced weapons were going to be their ticket to freedom.

Chapter Seven

Rezmona was still raging when she reached her chambers. Not noticing Gregor was waiting within, she let her power whip through the air, enjoying the release as things smashed against the walls.

"What has happened?" Gregor asked, announcing his presence. She should have known he'd be waiting for her. With his powers of foresight, he always knew when something was wrong.

"Nothing! Nothing happened," she screamed as a chaise lounge flew across the room. "I was finishing my inspections and when I came to the last group of prisoners my magick failed me."

Gregor hadn't moved from his seat in the corner, but the tension radiating off of him was hard to miss. He was smart to gauge his response, because one wrong move and she'd turn her anger on him. "Did something happen that was out of the ordinary, or could it just be that with the amount of prisoners we're processing this trip, your breeding magick has become depleted?"

Still breathing heavily from the anger coursing through her, Rezmona replied, "I'm not sure. I did enter the last cell planning to punish a prisoner, but I don't see how that could've affected my magick." She paused as inspiration hit. "Unless the cell was somehow warded."

"I'll have it inspected right away," Gregor replied.

* * * * *

Once Gregor left the queen's chambers, he went directly to the study and straight to the place where he'd hidden the book.

He felt that what happened to Rezmona's magick had more to do with the actual prisoners than the cell they were being kept in. But, he wasn't prepared to tell Rezmona of his ponderings just yet; first, he needed to finish the book to confirm his suspicions.

So far he'd discovered that the village was overflowing with abundance: rich soil, healthy townsfolk, and plentiful crops that kept the village overflowing with prosperity. But he hadn't reached a point in the book to explain exactly why.

After two hours of reading through strained eyes, Gregor finally found what he was looking for. The book described a prophecy of a recurring connection that allowed a spirit woman to draw on the magickal vortex beneath the village in order to sustain its prosperity. Gregor was now convinced that one of the women in that cell must be this spirit woman.

He gathered the book in his robes and began to make his way to the dungeon. Killing this woman was something that needed to be done. The book explained that not only was she the keeper of prosperity and abundance, but also their protector. This *prophecy's child* was their warrior, and that made her a threat.

When Gregor's foot touched the stone steps that led to the dungeon, he was hit with a vision of Rezmona lying on the ground with a knife in her chest. Stopping dead in his tracks, he tried to focus on the vision, but it vanished just as fast as it had appeared. Shaken by the sight of his beloved queen lying dead, the urgency to find and kill this girl overwhelmed him.

He righted himself, then proceeded down the stairs with a plan already in place. He would cast another sleeping spell, then examine each girl. Though he hadn't come across anything in the manuscript about the chosen woman bearing a sign, it was often the case in situations such as this. The spirits had a tendency to mark those they blessed.

Once he found the girl with the spirit mark, he would quarantine her until he could figure out what to do. He would give his life to protect his queen, and if this woman had the potential to kill her, then she wasn't someone to underestimate.

As Gregor stepped off the last step, he motioned for the guard. "Are the women in the last cell awake?"

"No, your grace. They all fell asleep not long ago."

"Good," Gregor replied as he slapped the guard kindly on the shoulder.

As he crept forward quietly, he could feel traces of magick tingling up his arms. Confident the woman who could threaten their existence was indeed inside this cell, he walked closer, death his urgent goal. It was imperative to eliminate this threat, mainly because the queen had yet to use her magick to produce an heir. If Rezmona was killed, the magick necessary to fuel the breeding program would be lost, leaving their race to slowly dwindle and die.

He found the women sleeping just as the guard had indicated. Raising his staff, he chanted under his breath, then watched as the familiar gray haze settled over the women. Though they were already sleeping, he could see the spell taking effect. He motioned to the guard to open the door and stepped inside with an evil grin on his face.

After casting the spell to create the enchanted weapons, Kylie could feel her energy starting to wane. Working magick, especially magick this powerful, definitely took a toll. She knew sleep was the only way to replenish her reserves. So, after giving thanks, closing her circle, and passing each woman their new weapon, they all laid down to get some much needed rest.

Reaching the point of relaxation didn't take long, but before Kylie could cross into the land of dreams, she felt the tingling of magick along her skin. As she tried to open her eyes, she was surprised when the spirits forced them to remain shut. Instead, they opened her third eye which allowed her to view the scene from within their realm.

Through her clairvoyance, see saw the old demon standing outside their cell. She heard him whisper a chant, then watched from the astral plane as the same gray haze she'd witnessed before seep from his staff and drift in their direction.

Her first instinct was to rise up against him, but as the thought entered her mind, she knew it was the wrong thing to do. Instead, she remained calm and pretended to sleep. Even as she watched the gray mist settle over her physical form, she knew the spell wouldn't work on her this time.

Through her mind's eye, she saw the demon enter the cell and kneel down next to Reni. With a vile look on his face he rolled her onto her stomach then grabbed a handful of hair, lifting it to inspect her neck. Next he moved to her arms and legs, taking the time to raise each one and look at every inch, even the soles of her feet. When he started to unzip the back of Reni's dress, Kylie truly started to panic.

The idea of this foul man undressing her friends and continuing his inspection in the most intimate of places had Kylie's rage boiling over. But suddenly, praise the gods, he stopped.

Kylie watched as he bent closer to Reni's back, and then with a raspy cry declared, "Yes!"

As he started to rise, Kylie caught a faint glimpse of what had excited him. She saw a spiral tattoo on Reni's left shoulder blade. The same tattoo that had formed on her palm earlier that night.

Kylie watched as the spirit realm caused her arm to flop over, revealing the same image to the old demon's eyes. He almost tripped over her arm, and therefore couldn't miss the symbol that glared up at him from her palm.

The demon's lips quivered with a snarl as he roughly grabbed at Kylie's hand and closely examined the mark. Reaching back to Reni's shoulder, he ran his fingers along the tattoo, striking her when he realized the two symbols were identical. "Damn!"

Watching him strike her friend had Kylie ready to fight, but the thought was pointless since she was still being held in this alternate state. Just as she began to struggle internally, she felt a shock to her system and was suddenly flooded with a sense of understanding.

The spirits had marked each of the women in an effort to hide Kylie's true identity. They had just saved her from being discovered as the prophecy's child.

Gregor was pleased when he spotted a spiral mark glaring up at him from the slave's shoulder. But just as he stood to motion to the guard, he tripped over another woman's outstretched arm, and found himself staring down at an exact replica of the mark.

Once he examined the tattoo on the slave's palm, he ran his fingers over the mark on the other girl's shoulder. "Damn!" he cried as he slapped the girl's back. The marks were identical.

He quickly examined the remaining slaves and realized that each of them had the exact same mark, only in different locations. He was so angry he couldn't contain the scream in his throat. Kicking the slaves from his path, he made his way back to the cell door.

"Do not let anyone enter this cell, and do not remove the prisoners from within," Gregor instructed the guard. "I'll return shortly."

Frustrated by his failure, he headed back towards his quarters contemplating exactly how he was going to keep Rezmona away from these particular slaves until he had a chance to finish the book. He was hoping the location of the prophecy child's mark would be included somewhere within the text.

When Gregor reached his chambers, he was coursing with energy. His senses were forcing him to finish the book, as his mind focused on the pleasure he'd receive by killing this girl. He lifted his hand and sent dark red sparks into the hearth, igniting the fire, then settled in for a long night of reading.

CHAPTER ELEVEN

Rezmona awoke feeling recharged and refreshed. *This is the perfect day to start the impregnations*, she thought to herself. Usually, they waited until all the prisoners were transported back to Abrinthill, but with the size of the castle and the extended timetable for their stay, she didn't see any reason not to start the process here.

Excited to share her plans with Gregor, she headed for his chambers.

Knocking once and receiving no response, she entered the room. "Gregor? Where are you?" Met with silence, she began scanning the room, frustration starting to build.

There was a fire in the hearth slowly dying out, a slew of papers scattered across the brocade couch, and an almost empty chalice of wine sitting on the desk next to that old tattered book.

Frowning at the sight of the book, Rezmona started to walk towards the desk but was stopped by Gregor's sudden appearance.

* * * * *

"Rezmona!" Gregor exclaimed, sounding startled. "I'm sorry, my Queen, I didn't hear you come in."

Gregor hastily made his way from the door of his bed chamber over to the desk. He watched as Rezmona's eyes narrowed when he quickly snatched up the book, returning it to the confines of his robe.

"Dammit, Gregor! What is it about that book that has you so engrossed?"

"Nothing in particular, my Queen. I'm sorry if my reading offends you, but in order to keep you safe and our breeding program uninterrupted, I feel it's important to learn all we can about the villages we raid."

He hoped his answer wasn't a bit too strained for Rezmona to take at face value, and was quickly relieved when she shrugged it off and said, "Speaking of the breeding program, I've decided to start the impregnations here in the castle. There is plenty of room, and if we are going to stay here to collect more prisoners, then I see no reason to wait. We don't want to get behind with the delivery schedule."

"I think that's a great idea. I'll have the guards prepare a makeshift birthing facility, and then we can begin to move the prisoners. Just leave everything to me." Gregor was relieved to have the attention directed away from his book and how her magick had failed. But his relief was short-lived as Rezmona continued.

"What did you find out from inspecting the prisoners' cell?" she asked.

Gregor internally debate whether he should lie to his queen in order to keep her safe. It didn't take him long to decide. "I found that the cell does indeed have special wards on it. I've instructed the guards to leave the prisoners as they are until I have a chance to remove them."

"Thank you, Gregor. We'll start the impregnations with the other prisoners and leave those few until last. That should give you plenty of time to remove the wards and allow me to perform the inspections. Now, I'll be in the garden if you need me."

Gregor bowed to the queen, then exhaled the breath he was holding once she left the room. He was confident that within the next few hours he would be able to find and kill the prophecy's child.

Chapter Twelve

After the spirit realm released Kylie, she fell back into a deep sleep—one that would replenish her severely drained energy reserves. The next morning, she woke to the sounds of scuffling coming from the other cells. She slowly scooted towards the bars to get a better view, then watched in horror as the other women were being taken by huge, bulging demons with engorged privates. The looks on their faces had her stomach twisting in knots. It looked as though each demon was choosing his preferred partner.

Kylie fell to the side and vomited, causing one of the demons to look her way. Panic filled her chest and she quickly felt for the magickal weapon that was tied to the inside of her gown. The feeling of the stone knife in her hand immediately calmed her nerves. She looked away from the demon to gaze at her friends and quickly realized they were still being held under by the old man's sleeping spell.

After watching all the demons grab their chosen women and leave the dungeon, Kylie knew it was time to make their move.

She crawled back to the spot where she'd previously cast her circle and once again began to call on her magick. "Spirit realm come to me, show me what I need to see. Guide me through the steps to take, to free these women and make our break."

The image that rose up in her mind's eye was one of her standing over the women with her hands extended. She moved over to them and did exactly what the vision had shown her. Opening her mouth the words that tumbled out weren't her own, even though it was her voice echoing through the cell. "Dark magick dissipate, allow these women to truly wake. The spirit realm protects these four, as our chosen child leads them out the door."

Kylie opened her eyes to see a bright gold healing light emanating from her hands. As soon as it enveloped the women, they began to stir. Kylie quickly gave her thanks and closed her circle.

"Friends, please wake. Our time to move has come." Kylie shook each of them in an effort to jolt them out of their spellbound slumber.

Standing at the cell's door, Kylie simply placed the pointed end of her blade into the lock. She and all the women watched as a surge of energy ran down her arm and out the end of the blade, lighting up each stone on the hilt as it passed through them.

The cell's door sprung open and the women all crept behind Kylie in a straight line down the corridor towards the stairs.

Kylie had a clear vision of where to go to make their escape, but as easy as it looked in her mind, she knew it wouldn't be so in reality.

Once they hit the top of the stairs, they all crouched down until Kylie gave the signal to move. All five women crept along the cold stone wall as they made their way through the empty corridor. When they reached the end of the hall, Kylie paused, placing her hands on the massive wooden door. After a moment of quiet meditation, she nodded her head and pulled on the large iron handle.

The door quietly swung open, revealing a massive ballroom, and the women rushed inside. Shaking from their fear of being discovered, they all stayed huddled together and waited for Kylie to indicate their next move. Once she verified it was clear, they raced across the large room to the door on the opposite wall. Through her visions, Kylie knew beyond this door was a long hallway which led to the main entrance and the front exit of the castle, but the multiple doors that lined the hall had Kylie very concerned. She knew once they passed this point, running into the demons was an obstacle they couldn't avoid.

Kylie placed her hand on the massive wrought iron handle, but as she started to pull, she caught sight of a small door off to the side of the room. It was made of glass and framed within a wall of windows, blending perfectly and making it hard to see. She motioned for the women to follow her as she made her way over to examine the alternate exit. Pressing her face against the glass door, Kylie cupped her hands around her eyes to give herself a better view against the glare.

"This leads to the garden, and from there we can hopefully find an exit onto the main grounds. Just let me check with the spirit realm to see if it's a safe alternative."

As Kylie prepared to enter her meditative state, there was a loud bang on the door they had just vacated. All the women squealed and started to glance back and forth with panicked looks on their faces.

"It seems as though we have no choice," Kylie announced. She opened the glass door and hurried everyone into the garden.

CHAPTER THIRTEEN

As Rezmona continued her stroll through the castle's lush landscape, she reminded herself to make a point of thanking Gregor for moving them here. Not only was it easily defendable, but it also offered many alternatives to fill her time with pleasant things. Even though she was the feared demon queen, she also appreciated things like the beautiful roses she was currently running the palm of her hand across. Things like the skillfully crafted stone benches that littered the garden, creating several intimate seating areas throughout. Things like...*what the hell?*

Rezmona froze as she tried to process what she was seeing. Five slave women sneaking out the side door of the castle into her garden? It couldn't be. No way would her warriors or Gregor let something like this happen. It just wasn't possible.

She continued to watch, thinking that perhaps it was a vision of things to come, or maybe her magick was showing her what the prisoners were planning. But when she finally caught sight of the prisoner's face who was leading them along the stone wall, Rezmona recognized her as the impudent slave from the dungeon. As the anger settled in her chest, she knew what she was seeing was truly happening.

"Stop!" Rezmona roared.

CHAPTER FOURTEEN

As soon as Kylie and the other women made their way into the beautiful garden, she spotted a wooden door at the far end of the stone wall. Kylie lifted her finger to her lips, then nodded her head towards the door. But, as soon as they began to creep along the wall they heard the most terrifying thing.

"Stop!"

Gripped by fear at the sound of the queen's voice echoing through the air, the women dropped to the ground. All except Kylie.

"How did you get out here? Never mind, because you're not going to live long enough to tell me."

As the queen's words registered, Kylie knew this was the moment that would decide the fate of her and her friends. They would either die by the queen's magick, or fight using their enchanted weapons and make their escape.

"Ready your weapons," Kylie instructed.

Kylie heard the women reach for their knives as she pulled her own from the confines of her dress. The smile on the evil queen's face was twisted and frightening, indicating she didn't see any of them as a threat. Kylie didn't let that distract her as she began to call on her magick.

"Spirit realm, please fill me, protecting these women is my duty. Give me the strength of your magick and will, to take down the Queen of Abrinthill."

The magick that surged through Kylie radiated around her in a blue mystical light. Her knife was pulsing with green earth energy as the stones lit up and glowed as brightly as the demon queen's red eyes.

The cackling laughter that spilled from Rezmona's lips was disturbing but Kylie stood her ground as the queen said, "Your magick is no threat to me. I will kill you where you stand."

"Then know it's my destiny to not only stop you, but to destroy you," Kylie replied.

The queen screamed so loud that the windows surrounding the garden shattered into a million pieces, forcing the cowering women to cover their heads. Kylie then watched as Rezmona dropped her glamour, revealing the demon she truly was.

Her towering red form was definitely intimidating, and her shiny black horns looked beautiful and deadly at the same time. Preparing herself for the ultimate fight, one she wasn't convinced she'd win, Kylie faced the queen, then ran to meet her fate.

The moment the two collided, Rezmona screeched in pain. The blue light surrounding Kylie was apparently like acid to the demon queen's skin, as spots on her arms started to bubble and ooze.

Kylie smiled, but then the queen jumped back out of her reach and quickly began to chant. "Dark magick come to me, punishing these women is what needs be. Fill my veins with your deadly power, for they shall die from where they cower."

The queen's normal magick wouldn't work against Kylie, so as the black tendrils started to encase her entire body, it was clear Rezmona was calling on the dark magick she used for the breeding program. Soon Rezmona was surrounded by black tendrils that were meant to be her protection as well as Kylie's death.

"You won't win that easily, slave," Rezmona threatened.

The queen charged forward and this time made contact without any pain. She punched Kylie in the stomach, sending her flying into the air, only to be slammed back down to the ground by one of the queen's dark tendrils that was now wrapped around her ankle. Kylie looked down at her leg and watched as the black satin looking ribbon of magick started winding its way higher and higher.

Using her knife, Kylie quickly sliced through the corporeal magick and watched as the inky black strand withered and disappeared. The queen froze in shock as Kylie taunted, "It appears none of your magick is strong enough to defeat me."

Kylie didn't wait for a response but instead threw herself at the queen. She punched and kicked like a true warrior, waiting for the perfect opening. After landing a solid hit to the queen's face and a kick to her gut, Kylie launched herself into the air, coming down atop the queen and burying her knife deep within her chest.

Kylie stood back and watched as the black magick that encased the queen's body started to shrink and squeeze, disintegrating until only two black and gold striped horns were left lying on the ground.

As the women rushed forward, their knives still tightly grasped in their hands, Kylie received another vision. The women looked the same, only bigger, and wore warrior gear which included their enchanted knives. The vision showed Kylie leading them into multiple battles and victories.

Suddenly, being prompted by the spirits themselves, Kylie reached down and grabbed one of Rezmona's horns, watching as the other dissolved into the earth.

The women gasped as she turned around and touched the horn to Lucy's, then Reni's heart. What happened next was the beginning of history itself.

Kylie watched as each of the women she touched with the demon horn grew to an incredible size. Almost double their original stature. Their clothes ripped and molded themselves into the warrior gear Kylie had seen in her vision; bra-like tops with bands crisscrossing their breasts, and fitted skirts with belts and weapons hanging from their waists.

She completed the process by touching Avetta, Trina, and then herself.

Kylie ended up being the largest of them all. Her beautiful black hair whipped in the wind as the demon horn shrank to a smaller size which then fit perfectly into a loop on her skirt.

Just as Kylie saw the old cloaked demon, followed by a wall of warriors coming out the garden door, everything around them started to disappear.

The women scrambled to their feet, only to find their toes buried in the sand.

"Kylie, where in the world are we?" Avetta asked.

Being guided by the spirits once again, Kylie answered. "We're on the island of Themiscyra in Ovialell. Welcome to your new lives."

And so, the day the demon queen died was the same day the Amazons were born.

Look for Kylie and her Amazons throughout the Ovialell series.

Tish Thawer

TISH THAWER

THE
RISE of RAE

~ An Ovialell Series Companion ~

THE RISE OF RAE

by

Tish Thawer

Inlavey was the city of the fae. Located on Upper World of Ovialell, it was home to the great fairy spirits, and watched over by the Goddess Diana.

Raeanne loved her home town. It was the greatest city in Ovialell as far as she was concerned. The villages were full of fun loving fairies and wandering through the magickal forests by fairy light, was one of her favorite things to do.

But unfortunately, Raeanne was an outcast.

She didn't look any different than the other fairies in her village, didn't act different, or talk different. But she *was* different. A one of a kind original...and she hated it.

It seemed so silly, but everyone she'd ever met made such a huge deal about her name that she'd begged her parents to change it at least a million times.

All of her "friends" had names like Brandi, Candi, Lindsy, Traci, or Kary. As a matter of fact, *all* female fairies had names that ended in "i" or "y." It was the way of her people, a time honored tradition, as it was thought the females of their race forged a special connection to the fair"y" spirits through their names. So when her parents decided to name her Raeanne, they had basically ruined her life.

Her mother and father, Sari and Venrick, explained they'd been led by the fairy spirits to name her as they did and breaking tradition wasn't something that had been easy for them. But if you were lucky enough to receive a message from the spirits...it was something you didn't ignore.

"Rae, are you going to town today or would you like to help me do the baking?" her mother asked.

"I'll help you, Mama. You know I don't like going into town." Raeanne tied up her long brown hair before reaching for the wooden mixing bowls.

"Have you been having more trouble?" Sari asked.

Rae closed her eyes and took a deep breath. How was she suppose to explain to her mother that it was all her fault? That every time she went to town she had trouble. She was teased, made fun of, pushed around, and most often...simply ignored. She knew it would hurt her mama to hear such things, but at the same time, she didn't want to lie to her.

"It's alright, Mama. I'm used to it. Besides, once I turn eighteen next month and complete my fairy trial, hopefully people will stop harassing me about my name."

She tried to smile as she turned back to the table, but her mother's knowing stare had her blinking away tears.

"Raeanne. You are a special girl with a special name. And I have no doubt that once your trial is complete, you'll finally have some clarity as to just how special you are."

Her mom kissed her on the cheek, tucked a stray strand of hair behind her ear, and then blew a puff of flour straight into her face.

"Mama!" Rae exclaimed. Sari laughed and continued to gather the ingredients for the baked goods they'd be preparing today.

Raeanne put on her fur boots and wool cape, then gathered the warm rolls and loafs of bread into her basket before heading to the door.

"Be safe, darling. Dinner will be ready when you return," her mother said.

Rae was headed to town after all, as the extra baked goods they made would garner a good price when sold fresh at the market.

"Don't worry, Mama. I'll be back soon."

Raeanne took a deep breath, enjoying the feel of the crisp winter air, then started down the cobblestone path that led from her house to the center of town. She kept her head down and walked with feather light steps as mature fairies flew around while youngsters ran by playing, their laughter filling the air.

She almost made it to the baker when she felt someone creeping up behind her. Suddenly, her basket was knocked to the ground. She watched the bread roll into the ditch before turning around to look the hoodlums in the face.

"Freak!" they yelled.

She stared coldly at their backs as they ran away. She learned long ago that fighting back, or trying to defend herself, only made things worse.

She felt ashamed as she wiped a lone tear from her cheek, since she'd just told her mother she was use to being picked on. It looks like she lied to her after all.

Just as she began to gather the bread, as not to leave a mess on the side of the road, she heard, "Here, let me help you."

It's wasn't just the male voice that startled her, but the actual offer of help, as it was something that had never happened before.

Raeanne looked up and was met with the sweetest smile and a stunning pair of cerulean blue eyes.

"Hi. I'm Prayter," said the attractive male fairy. He used his powerful wings to speed from one discarded loaf of bread to another, gathering all the spilled contents of her basket within seconds.

Dropping her eyes to the ground she quickly replied, "Thank you." As she turned to walk away, Prayter tapped her on the shoulder.

"May I walk you home?"

Her anxiety spiked and she yelled, "Leave me alone!" She took off running, but with the force of his wings, Prayter appeared in front of her a second later.

Holding up his hands, he pleaded, "Wait. Please. I just want to talk to you."

"Why? So you can pretend to be nice to the freak, then attack her in the woods, or something like that?"

Prayter sucked in a breath and his brow developed a deep

crease. "Why would you say that? I would never hurt you. And why would you call yourself a freak?"

Raeanne took a moment to really look at Prayter and realized she'd never seen him before. She'd lived in this village her whole life, so the fact that she didn't recognize him meant he wasn't from around here. So instead of answering his question, she asked one of her own instead. "Where are you from?"

"I'm from Bhrnmar, it's three villages over from Inlavey. Have you never been?"

She shook her head, her eyes darting to the ground once again. "Well, trust me when I tell you, walking me home would be bad for your health," Rae explained.

Patting himself on the chest, Prayter smiled. "Well, I'm in pretty good shape, so I think I'll take my chances."

Prayter boldly reached out and took her hand, not waiting for a response. But the one he got probably wasn't at all what he expected.

The rapid pounding of her heart had Raeanne feeling as though it was about to burst from her chest.

This was the first time in her entire life that someone other than her parents had risked touching her since she was practically viewed as a leper. For someone like Prayter to show her such kindness...it was simply more than her raw nerves could handle.

Tears streamed down her face as she stood frozen, staring at the intersection where their fingers intertwined.

"I'm sorry. I...um...I didn't mean to upset you," Prayter said.

He tried to release her hand, but her muscles seized, and her brain suddenly lost ability to make her fingers move. They stood frozen, like a statue of two lovers holding hands, while happy tears escaped her.

When she finally quieted, Prayter wiggled his fingers free of her grasp. "Um...sorry, but my hand's falling asleep."

Rae released a nervous giggle as she flexed her hand, then quickly used her now functioning fingers to wipe the wet streaks from her cheeks. "I'm so sorry. It's just...I've never had anyone touch me before."

The confused look on his face confirmed he was definitely not from around here. Because anyone from this village knew that to touch her, the *freak*, was to risk losing your connection to the spirit world. At least that was the vicious rumor someone had started when she was a baby.

"I don't understand," Prayter said. "Exactly how old are you?"

"Seventeen. I turn eighteen and will face my trial next month."

"Then explain to me how, in your seventeen years, no one has ever touched you?"

Rae sighed and her eyes darted around, looking for something to focus on as she tried to think of a rational response. She considered lying to him, but the thought was fleeting, as she knew he would discover her secret soon enough. So instead, she simply replied, "My name is Raeanne."

CHAPTER FIVE

Raeanne. Prayter let the name roll around in his head, not understanding the buzzing sensation it seemed to cause.

"That's a beautiful name," he replied. "But it doesn't explain why no one has ever touched you."

"It should. My name is not traditional, and therefore people see me as an outcast. They think I'm evil and are scared I'll sever their connection to the fairy spirits." She shook her head at her own admission, then without warning grabbed his arm in a firm grip. "As you can see, it's completely untrue, but no one outside my family has ever risked touching me...until you. Thank you for putting that rumor to rest."

She flung his arm away as if it stung her hand, then began to walk away, her footsteps stomping heavily on the ground.

Flapping his wings to keep pace with her, Prayter asked, "Have I angered you?"

Shooting a quick glance over her shoulder, she replied, "No. But it just proves how wrong all the people in my village have been for seventeen years, and *that* makes me angry."

He didn't blame her for feeling slighted. He couldn't imagine being treated so poorly for something as simple as your name. But then again, the males of the fairy world didn't carry as strong of a connection to the spirits as the females. He could admit that Raeanne was definitely not a traditional fairy name, but for some reason, the effect it had on him was obviously not the same as it had on others.

"Well, maybe it's because I'm not from here, but I don't think you're evil, or an outcast, or a freak. I actually think your beautiful and unique. I'll bet that when you complete your trial, you'll develop the most stunning pair of wings and have some really powerful magick. And with that being said, I would still love to walk you home if you'd let me."

The fairy trial was something that all mature fairies had to face. Once they completed the tasks assigned, they would receive their wings and magick, taking their place as full-fledge fairies.

Prayter had just completed his trial this past Christmas, as every trial takes place on Christmas Eve, ending the following day. Unbeknownst to the human world, a successful trial contributed to their "white Christmases," because only when a fairy got their wings and magick, did humans get snow on Christmas day.

At his heartfelt proclamation, Raeanne stopped dead in her tracks, causing him to do the same. He hoped he hadn't been too forward, but at this point he didn't care. From the moment he felt the odd sensation which pulled him from his home two days ago, drawing him to Inlavey, he knew there was a special reason he was here. The instant he saw Raeanne...he knew *she* was that special reason.

"You still want to walk me home? Why? Why risk your safety or status while visiting Inlavey by being seen with me?"

"I'm not worried about my status or my safety, but I am worried about yours. I feel drawn to you, and I don't care what other people think about you and your odd name, I like you," he declared.

The smile that spread across Raeanne's face had him confident he'd said the right thing. The feeling was confirmed when she reached back and grabbed his hand once more, giving it a slight squeeze.

Raeanne listened to Prayter explain that he didn't care what other people thought of her, and that he felt drawn to her in some special way, and right now, as they held hands again, she had the exact same feeling.

"Where are you staying during your visit to Inlavey?" she asked.

Kicking a stone from their path, Prayter answered, "I'm not sure. I just got here."

"Well, I don't think my parents will let you stay with us, but you're more than welcome to stay for dinner." Rae smiled, reveling in the moment.

Having someone to talk to and hold hands with was a small miracle in itself, but having a handsome, kind, and funny male fairy show her this level of attention was truly a feat of the Gods.

"Thank you. Dinner sounds like a great place to start," Prayter replied.

As they made their way around the final curve of the stone path that led back to Rae's house, she loosened her grip. The small *humph* that escaped Prayter embarrassed her, since it was obvious her action meant she didn't want her family to see them holding hands.

"I'm sorry. It's just that I'm not sure how my parents are going to react to me bringing home a stranger, let alone, one I'm holding hands with."

"It's alright. I understand," Prayter replied.

But what happened next was beyond either of their understanding.

Raeanne's father came racing out the door, waving frantically in their direction.

"Rae, hurry. Something wonderful is happening."

With a quick glance at each other, they both sprinted towards her house.

When they entered the living room her father slapped Prayter on the shoulder as if they'd known each other forever.

Rae would have questioned the gesture if her attention wasn't fixed on the portal shimmering in the corner of the room and the old fairy standing beside it.

"Raeanne, I'm glad you're back. My name is Manix and I'm a member of the fairy council. I was just explaining to your parents that the time to fulfill your destiny has come."

"My *destiny*? But my trial isn't for another month." She sat the bread basket on the floor, then wiped her sweaty palms on her skirt.

"You're trial became irrelevant the moment you met your Hand."

The confusion layering her mind was so thick that words completely escaped her.

Thankfully Prayter spoke up instead. "Her *Hand*?" he questioned.

Manix gestured to the couch and waited as they all took their seats.

"The fairy spirits came to your parents when you were born with a special request of what to name you. It was done so because you, Raeanne, are to be our first queen."

The gasps that filled the room were the only interruption to Manix's story. "The fairy spirits have been led by the Goddess Diana to name a queen who can lead our people. When you were conceived, your energy was fused with the silver magick of the fairy realm. "Your Hand," he gestured to Prayter, "was also chosen by the spirits to be your mate."

With eyes wide, Rae stared at Prayter with a new sense of wonder, amazed by the silver streaks that were currently threading their way through his hair.

When a mature fairy completed their trial, the magick that took root as they received their wings displayed as streaks throughout their hair. Anyone with water magick developed blue streaks, earth magick presented as green streaks, and spirit magick showed as silver, which held the highest connection to the fairy realm.

"Queen? My daughter is going to be the first fairy queen?" Her mother's voice was quivering and tears filled her eyes as Raeanne moved to comfort her.

Manix interrupted their tender moment by saying, "Raeanne. Now that you've found Prayter, all you need to do is enter the portal to claim your destiny as our queen."

The moment Rae and Prayter stepped out of the portal, the landscape had them both gasping for breath. They stood frozen as they stared at the most beautiful castle, rising higher than the eye could see, against the brilliant blue sky.

Raeanne squealed and threw herself into Prayter's arms, as her mother, father, and Manix emerged from the portal.

"This is a gift from the fairy spirits. The official castle of the Seelie Fae Queen. Welcome to your new home, Raeanne."

"This is just so unreal. How can I be the Queen? I don't even have my magick or my wings."

Manix walked towards the front of the castle, motioning for them all to follow.

"All you have to do is enter your castle to claim your destiny and take your place as our Queen."

Rae bit her lip as she looked between her mother and father, then turned to Prayter, who gave her a reassuring nod.

As Rae placed her hand on the large iron handle of the intricately carved wood door, a tingling sensation rushed through her entire body. As the door suddenly began to glow, Rae was lifted into the air, her body engulfed in a brilliant silver light. She could feel her wings beginning to form, and the amount of magickal energy coursing through her was so intense it was as if the Gods where actually touching her.

As she floated softly to the ground she found her parents staring at her with tears in their eyes and a sense of wonder on their faces.

"Mama, what's wrong?"

"Raeanne. You're so...beautiful." Her mother covered her mouth in an effort to hold back her soft sobs.

Rae turned to Prayter and found him wearing a similar expression. Manix motioned for her to turn again towards the castle door. What she found had her joining the others in a feeling of disbelief.

The door was now a mirror, and the image she saw reflected was that of a beautiful full-fledged fairy with pure silver hair, and the most amazing pair of large white sparkling wings. They shimmered as if they were coated in diamonds, reaching far above her head and down to just inches above the ground.

Before she could say a word, the door returned to its wooden state as Manix spoke again. "Within this castle you'll find many wonders, but one of the most enchanted is this special door. It has been forged from the Rune Tree, and will always protect you from those who pass through it. This is just one of the many gifts the spirits have bestowed upon you, Raeanne."

Rae pushed off the ground and felt as though flying was the most natural thing in the world. She hoped that being Queen would come just as easily.

Before Manix disappeared back through the portal he held out his hand and smiled as the first flakes of pure white snow fell into his palm. Bowing, he said, "Take the next month to make this castle your home, for on Christmas day there will be a celebration in your honor. The Rise of Rae, the first Queen of the Fae."

Look for mention of Raeanne throughout the Ovialell series.

Tish Thawer

TISH THAWER

Shay
AND THE
BOX *of* NYE

~ An Ovialell Series Companion ~

Shay and the Box of Nite

by

Tish Thawer

Shay jumped from her bed and ran to the calendar that hung on the wall of her room. December twenty-fourth. She stared at the date, double checking to make sure it wasn't just wishful thinking.

"Yes!"

She ran from her bedroom, her gauzy blue nightgown billowing behind her as she made her way down the small spiral staircase that led to the kitchen.

"Mama, my trial starts today. I'm so nervous." She sat down at the table and scooped herself a portion of berry and cinnamon oatmeal from the large pot in front of her, then continued, "Can you give me some hints or tell me what yours was like?"

"Don't be nervous, Shay. The fairy trial is something every mature fairy has to go through. I can't tell you anything about my trial though, because if you're successful in retrieving the Box of Nye, part of the process is that the memories of what you faced during your trial are completely erased. This happens as you receive your wings and complete the transformation into a full-fledge fairy."

"Really? You don't remember anything at all?"

"No, honey. I sure don't." Narine turned off the stove and took a seat next to her oldest daughter. "Just follow the rules, and prepare for the unexpected." She kissed Shay on the forehead and moved to exit the room. "I'll leave you alone to get ready. The fairy council will be here shortly to go over everything. Good luck, honey. I know you'll do great."

Shay finished her oatmeal as she pondered her mother's words, *"Prepare for the unexpected."*

"How the heck am I suppose to do that?" she asked out loud. The whole point of something being unexpected is that you *can't* prepare for it.

This definitely didn't help put her mind at ease, but she knew dwelling on the what if's wasn't an option. She placed her wooden bowl in the sink and headed back upstairs to get ready for the council's arrival.

As she entered her bedroom, a feeling of peace settled over her. She was so grateful she finally had a space to herself——one that she didn't have to share with her younger sisters any more. When Shay reached maturity at the age of eighteen, her mom and dad had used their fairy magick to expand their treetop home, creating a beautiful bedroom and bathroom just for her. The ceiling was lined with vines filled with fairy lights, and crystals of all colors shined from their facets within the walls.

Shay stared at her reflection in the mirror as the tub began to fill. She noticed her skin was shimmering a little brighter than usual, and her long platinum hair was starting to develop streaks of blue and silver throughout. Looking into her own sapphire colored eyes, she smiled. The process of becoming a full-fledge fairy had already begun.

Each fairy develops a specific set of magick during their transformation, and as Shay stared at the blue and silver steaks weaving their way through her hair, she couldn't have been happier. Blue meant that she'd be able to control water and emotions, and silver was a link to their Queen and the divine fairy spirits. Silver was rare magick within their clan, and meant someday she would have the potential of becoming Queen, as only those with silver magick had the necessary link to the fairy spirits required to take a royal position.

Shay slipped off her nightgown and stepped into the steaming bath, allowing herself to appreciate the relaxing lavender aroma that was a constant in any bathroom across their land. If you ran water in a kitchen it always smelled like citrus; if you ran water outside it smelled like fresh cut grass even if it was the dead of winter; but here in the bathroom it was always lavender laced.

Taking the time to let her muscles relax, Shay started to make a mental list of all the things she'd planned to take with her on the trial. Her leather vest, riding pants, and tall boots would be her chosen outfit, which was traditional. However, she planned to include a few extra things into the belt and pockets she'd added to her ensemble. Things like her favorite knife which was made from tampered steel that displayed a polished finish of rainbow colors; and the spell bottle she carried like a canteen which was a beautiful mix of blue, green, and purple glass. It was now filled to the brim with the potion she'd recently brewed for this specific day. For reasons beyond her understanding, she'd been guided in its creation and knew it was going to be something she would need.

Shay had been dreaming of and preparing for this day most of her teenage years, but now that it was upon her she couldn't help but wonder if she'd done enough.

Shay heard a knock on the front door just as she finished putting her knife in its sheath. Pulling her ponytail tight, she raced down the stairs to find her mother welcoming three members of the fairy council into their home.

"Good morning, gentlemen. Welcome to our home. May I present my daughter, Shay."

Shay bowed to the council members and waited for their acknowledgement before rising, as was custom.

"Rise, young Shay. Today is the day of your fairy trial. Your hunt for the Box of Nye will either end in triumph, in which case you will get your wings and take your place as a full-fledged fairy. Or it will end in disappointment, with you remaining wingless and without magick for the rest of your days."

Listening to them state the obvious set Shay's nerves on edge, but she showed no outward signs of emotion other than pure confidence.

"Gentlemen, I'll leave you alone to begin," said her mother. Then turning in her direction, Narine continued, "Shay, I love you and have full confidence in you. Be safe, and I can't wait to see your wings tomorrow on Christmas Day."

After receiving a kiss from her mother, Shay found herself alone in the kitchen with the three council members. They gestured towards the table and Shay quickly took a seat.

As the council members moved to join her, Shay studied each of the men closely. One was as old as you'd image Father Time to be, another was skinny and had a deteriorated look about him; like instead of aging, he was simply wasting away, but it was the last man who really caught her off guard.

Not only was he much, much younger than the other two, but after looking with a keener eye, she realized this man was her long lost friend, Joseph.

Not wanting to make a bad impression, she contained her surprise and continued her observations, but on the inside Shay was bursting with the need to jump into Joe's lap, wrap her arms around his neck, and then start badgering him with questions. Questions like: Where have you been the last few years? How did you join the council at such a young age? When are you going to kiss me again?

Okay, maybe that last one was out of line, but Joe had been the first boy that Shay had loved, and they'd spent an amazing eight months together. Then on Christmas Eve, three years ago, he'd completed his fairy trial and simply disappeared.

Switching her focus back to the man who was the obvious leader of the three, she noticed one last thing that stood out about them all. Each had red streaks throughout their hair. Red, and no other color, which was odd because most fairies develop two levels of magick. Red was the sign of fire magick and passion, and it was pretty obvious that this magick was the main requirement to becoming a council member.

"Shay, the rules of the fairy trial are simple. You will be given three items that you're required to find. These three items are the only way you'll find the location of the Box of Nye, but beware, finding them won't be an easy task. Your path will be fraught with danger and unexpected things that could lead you astray. Focus, remember your goal, and once all three items are brought together, the location of the box will be revealed. You'll have until midnight, at which time the box will reveal itself if you've completed your tasks, but if not...you will be transported back home to live out your life without wings or magick. Do you understand?"

"Yes, Sir."

"Do you have any questions for us?"

"Actually, yes. I would like to know if there are any other rules. Rules pertaining to what I can and cannot do during my trial."

All three of the council members smiled, and Shay was proud of herself for following her gut and asking the question.

"Yes. There is one other rule. No one else may help you on your quest."

"No one? Not even the fairy spirits themselves?"

The frowns that now replaced their smiles had Shay worried she'd overstepped her boundaries, but when they answered, her confidence was restored. "Of course the fairy spirits are allowed to help, not that they ever have or ever will."

Maybe Shay's confidence came from the silver magick building inside of her, she didn't know, but for some reason their answer had put a cocky smile on her face. "Thank you, gentlemen. I'm ready to begin."

Joseph spoke next, causing her smile to spread even wider. "The first item you'll need to find is the peach feather of a trig owl. As you know, trig owls are very rare, and so this is no easy task."

Shay simply nodded.

The skinny one spoke next. "The second item you'll need to acquire is a rasper shell from the Lake of Sorrow. As you know, the Lake of Sorrow is no playground, and so this is no easy task."

The old man spoke last. "The final item you'll need to find is the wooden key made from bark of the Rune Tree. As you know, the Rune Tree is sacred and protected, and so this is no easy task. But only with its key will you be able to find the Box of Nye."

Shay stood, bowed, and spoke the customary response. "I accept the challenge of my trial."

The council members all stood and bowed in return, then left without saying another word, but just as Joseph was shutting the door, Shay caught the quick smile and wink he sent her way. Feeling the heat rise in her cheeks, Shay smiled back and gave a little wave just as he shut the door, leaving her alone in the kitchen.

Shay immediately started to gather her supplies, packing a loaf of bayberry bread and a flask of herb laced wine into her travel satchel. She knew getting started on her quest as soon as possible was a necessity, but forced herself to take a moment to look around the small kitchen. She had to make sure she'd grabbed everything she would need, because the moment she stepped out her front door she'd be transported to her starting location.

Shay took one last look at their beautiful Christmas tree standing in the corner. It had silver and gold fairy lights woven through out, beautiful glass balls in all shapes and sizes, each with their own wintertime scene playing within, and a sparkling purple and silver ribbon wrapped around the entire thing. She couldn't wait to return home on Christmas Day and watch her sisters tear open their presents while she hovered in the corner using her newly developed wings. Yes, she was that confident she'd succeed.

All fairy trials took place on Christmas Eve, ending on Christmas Day. It'd probably be a big surprise for humans to find out that whenever they got snow on Christmas Day, it was only because another fairy had completed their trial and received their wings and magick.

Shay took a deep breath and opened the front door. Then, closing her eyes, she took a step over the threshold and straight into the portal. The first thing she felt was the change in temperature. It was warmer here...wherever *here* was. She slowly opened her eyes, finding herself forced to squint as the sun shone brightly in the sky. After placing her hand above her eyes, creating a shield from the blinding rays, the first thing Shay noticed was a large grove of swaying aspen trees. She knew instantly where she was, thanks to all the studying she'd done to prepare for this day. The only aspen grove in the land was on the far edge of the Feygan territory.

Her mind quickly ran through all she'd learned about this area. She knew the animals that resided here were not only rare, but extremely dangerous. Shay almost laughed out loud, as she contemplated the situation. Of course the trig owls would choose this as their home; they were flesh eating predators and would fit right in.

Shay didn't waste any time and started to move into the tree line. The moment she found herself surround by shimmering yellow leaves was also the moment she noticed multiple sets of red eyes hungrily staring at her. Realizing she wasn't the only one hunting for something in this grove, Shay reached for her knife. Suddenly a small, half-bird half-rodent looking creature came flying directly at her on wings made of scales and feathers. Unfortunately this wasn't the feather she needed, so her quick reaction was to slice through the creature's belly.

Twenty minutes later, after lots of slicing and dicing, Shay had made her way to the thickest part of the aspen grove. The trees here were so tall and thick they almost blotted out the sun. She searched the skies for any sign of a trig owl with no luck. The only things she saw were more beady eyes, and slivers of yellow as the aspen leaves floated on the breeze ever so often. After staring into the treetops for a good ten minutes with no results, Shay decided to give herself a break and took a seat on the ground. Leaning back against one of the tall trees she opened her flask and took a long drag of the herb laced wine. Feeling the exhaustion from her fight so far, she closed her eyes and took a deep breath.

As she relaxed while the healing wine did its job, she began contemplating what her next move should be. Should she climb one of the trees and look for a nest? Should she scour the ground and see if any fallen feathers were buried within the forest floor? She didn't know, but upon opening her eyes, all thoughts of the peach feather quickly fled her mind.

She now found herself staring at a group of the bird/rodent like creatures with their wings tucked in. They were using their tiny feet to sneak up on her instead. Shay jumped up, fumbling to unsheathe her knife, but unfortunately she wasn't quick enough. One of the small creatures launched itself at her leg and sunk its teeth into her flesh. She cried out and smacked it away, then sent it flying across the forest with a fierce kick. Shay held her position, ready for another attack, but was surprised when all the creatures started to scurry away. Suddenly, she heard a loud screech from above. Looking up, she saw a large owl swooping down towards her, riding wings made of peach feathers. The trig owl. She should have known...it was drawn to the blood that was currently running down her leg.

Shay stood her ground, knowing this was going to be her only chance. She had to let the owl get close enough to think it would be getting a taste of her flesh, and when the time was right, she'd grab the first item required by her trial...the peach feather.

Only seconds ticked by until the owl was within reach. As the predatory bird opened it mouth and bared its clawed talons at Shay, she ducked to the right while yanking one of the feathers from the tip of its wing. The owl let out another screech as it fell awkwardly to the ground. It wasn't hurt and the removal of one feather wasn't going to stop it from flying, so Shay took off at a dead run back towards the edge of the forest.

Shay didn't stop running until she reached the spot where she'd entered the Feygan territory. She watched the portal start to shimmer and vibrate the closer she got. With a quick glance back at the aspen grove, she stepped through the portal without a second thought.

Quickly taking in her new surroundings, Shay spotted the Lake of Sorrow. It was shining like a large piece of black onyx and sat at the bottom of the slope in front of her. She was thankful the portal was placing her in such convenient locations, because even though she'd packed all her maps and scrying tools weeks in advance, she really didn't want to use them to find her way if she didn't have to.

Checking the sun's position in the sky as she'd done since she was a little girl, she noted it was only eleven o'clock in the morning. She was happy with her progress since she'd retrieved the first item of her trial and it wasn't even noon.

Tucking the trig owl's feather into her satchel, Shay then started towards the lake, but after a few steps, the slope became increasingly steep. Slowing her pace didn't seem to help and suddenly she could hardly stop herself from sliding straight into the lake below. She sunk down to her bottom and dug in her heels. It slowed her progress by a fraction, but she still ended up sliding down the side of the hill, stopping just as her feet touched the edge of the lake.

Falling back onto the wet bank, she closed her eyes and let out a sigh of relief. The next sound that left Shay however wasn't relief, but instead, a scream. She bolted upright and started kicking at the gray slimy hands that were now wrapped around her ankles, pulling her into the lake.

In just moments, Shay had multiple hands wrapped around her legs. She started to reach for her knife, but quickly realized that could be a bad idea. If she were to miss her target and nail herself in the leg instead, she'd inflict an injury that would quickly bring her trial to an end.

So, as hard as it was, Shay tried to calm her movements as well as her mind. The first thing that happened was a tingling sensation that started from her head and ran through her entire body. She opened her mouth and said the words that had magickally formed in her mind. "I have no sorrow for this lake to claim. Release me now and I'll cast no blame."

Shay was relieved when the hands released her, but now found herself treading water, as the tingling from the magick strands in her hair started to subside. Even though she was no longer being tugged at, she could still feel the effects of the lake starting to seep into her soul. The cold feeling she was experiencing wasn't just from the frigid temperature of the water, but from the bone deep depression the lake caused in anyone who got too close.

She made her way to the shore and drug herself back onto the bank. Scooting up the slope as far as she could, Shay drew out the loaf of bayberry bread and her flask of wine again.

Taking a moment to gather her thoughts and regain some energy from the sustenance the bread and wine provided, she contemplated how in the world she was suppose to retrieve a shell from this lake when it was a black as coal and apparently filled with some seriously scary things.

She laughed at herself when the first thought she had was to fashion a wand out of one of the sticks lying on the bank and shout, "Accio rasper shell." Until her magick was fully in place she wouldn't be able to pull off something like that.

Stopped short by the thought of her magick and the tingling that was once again beginning to radiate from the strands in her hair, Shay dropped her bread and flask on the ground. She grabbed a handful of her hair and was mesmerized to see the blue strands sparking to life. The blue strands that carried her water magick.

Shay stood up and walked straight into the lake. Within seconds she was waist deep in the black water, but suddenly a blue light started to radiate from below the surface. Shay quickly realized that the light was coming from her. She closed

her eyes and let the magickal words fill her mind once again.

"Water is mine to command, rasper shell come, this I demand.

I take from these waters but leave a part of me, as I say it so

mote it be."

Using her knife, Shay sliced a thin line across her palm and

let her blood drip into the water as payment. Then she watched

as the rasper shell drifted up from the bottom of the lake and

straight into her hand.

Rejoicing that she now had two of the three items required

for her trial, she let out a loud "Whoop!"

Trudging from the lake and back up to the spot on the hill

where her items lay, Shay added the shell to her backpack and

sat down to finish her snack. But as she sat nibbling the bread

and sipping the wine, her joyous thoughts began to waver and

soon she felt tears streaming down her face. She was

overwhelmed with the sudden fear that this was too easy; that

she was succeeding now, only to fail the last task. What if she couldn't find the wooden key and never got her wings or felt her full magick coursing through her veins? Or never got the chance to become Queen of her fairy clan. It only took minutes before Shay was wracked with fear and curled up in a ball. She let the tears flow and she closed her eyes, accepting that she'd never complete her trial.

A strange sound woke Shay from the dead sleep she was currently in. She quickly sat up and took stock of her surroundings. She was still on the bank of the Lake of Sorrow, and it was almost dark. She had slid down the hill and was lying close to the water...a little too close for comfort.

Shay jumped up, quickly realizing what had happened. The lake's affect on her had caused the fears that led to her depressive sleep. Thank goodness for whatever sound had woken her, because she had a feeling if she'd remained unconscious for much longer, she would've ended up in the lake again, but this time, her stay would have been permanent.

Shay quickly gathered her things and fought her way back up the hill to where the portal awaited. Just as before, it shimmered and vibrated as she stepped through without hesitation.

Emerging on the other side, Shay found herself in a forest of the tallest evergreen trees she'd ever seen. They easily stretched one hundred feet into the air, filling the sky and filtering the sun. The rays of light illuminated the snow as if some of her fairy relatives had sprinkled it with silver glitter.

She recognized the area as the oldest forest in all of the land. Everyone knew this forest was home to the Rune Tree. This tree was worshiped by her clan and was protected by the fairy spirits.

When a fairy had an important question they would journey to the Rune Tree. After asking their question, they would watch as the runes carved into the tree trunk illuminated, therefore, providing them their answer. It technically worked just like rune stones, but thanks to the spirits, these runes were instead carved into a sacred tree.

The only problem at the moment was that Shay had never journeyed to the tree herself, and since she'd lost most of her day—thanks to her sorrowful nap—she had less time to find the tree...let alone the key.

Thinking it only made sense to head in the direction that was associated with the element of earth, Shay headed North. She travelled at a rapid pace, knowing when she found the Rune Tree there'd be no mistaking it.

As the last stream of sunlight disappeared and the moon rose in the sky, Shay was suddenly struck with the feeling that she was getting close. She quickened her pace and ran towards a large group of trees, and just as she emerged from the thick forest, she spotted the Rune Tree. Bathed in moonlight, it stood tall and beautiful in a small grove, and was unlike anything she'd ever seen. It was no evergreen, but instead, a large purple maple with shimmering leaves. Even in the dark, its leaves gave off a subtle lavender glow.

Smiling wide, Shay made her way to the boundary of the tree. She could feel the magickal barrier that protected it pushing gently against her hand as she reached out. She had no idea how she was going to find the wooden key made from its bark. As a matter of fact, when the old councilman mentioned it, that was the first time she'd ever heard of any such item. She didn't know if the key still resided as part of the tree itself, or was fashioned and then moved and hidden. She truly had no idea how to proceed.

Taking note of the moon's position, she knew it was almost 7 p.m., and that she only had five hours to complete her task. This was the moment she truly started to panic.

Shay walked around the tree again and again, trying to look at every inch of the trunk. Up and down, side to side, from the very roots up to as high as she could see, but found nothing. Not a strange notch or mark, not a weird scrape or cut, and definitely not a convenient key-shaped indention, but suddenly she had an idea. Why not use the tree for what it was meant for...receiving answers. She raised her arms and asked out loud, "Where can I find the wooden key made from the bark of your tree?"

She watched with anticipation, but when nothing happened she yelled out as she sank to the ground, "Come on!"

Feeling defeated, she laid back onto the soft mulch of the forest floor and stared into the starry sky. Blanking her mind, Shay let herself fall into the meditative state she'd practiced since she was a little girl. She felt herself floating, as if cradled by the hands of the fairy spirits themselves. She imagined the Rune Tree in her mind's eye, and suddenly knew just what to do.

Sitting up, she took note of the moon again and realized that too much time had passed while she'd been meditating for her answer. Though it'd only felt like minutes, receiving her vision had apparently taken over an hour, and it was now almost 9 p.m.

Shay rushed back to the barrier of the Rune Tree and focused her mind once more. She then asked her question by thinking the words, making sure they were laced with reverence. *Allow me to find the key I need, which will fulfill my destiny.*

The fairy Queen I will be, with your help...wise Rune Tree.

She watched as the runes on the tree started to glow. She quickly reached in her backpack and took out her journal and charcoal pencil. She took note of which runes lit up and in which order. And after the tree went back to normal, Shay settled back down on the ground and started studying her sketches.

The first rune represented East, the direction of the element of air, and inspiration. The second rune represented royalty, which was another sign Shay was destined to become the next Queen. The silver strands in her hair tingled at the thought, making her even more giddy. The third rune represented love, and the fourth represented things lost. She quickly puzzled out what it meant, knowing that she was being guided by the spirits themselves.

Excited to finish her trial and start the new life that was being laid out before her, Shay gathered her things and started running back towards the portal. She knew it'd be close to 11 p.m. when she reached her final destination and hoped that an hour was enough time to get to the Queen's castle.

After racing through the portal, Shay was filled with such satisfaction that her vision had been right, that she spun around and shouted, "Yes! Thank you, fairy spirits."

Sitting tall on the cliffs of Inlavey, the Queen's castle loomed in the East. She took off at a dead run and never let up until she was stood on the edge of a large chasm. It was as if the earth had split open just to stop her from finishing her trial.

Shay cursed her earlier enthusiasm as she tried to remain calm and figure out what to do. She looked left then right and noticed that the chasm narrowed in the far distance. She could barely see it and knew the time it would take to reach the end meant that she would not make it to the castle before midnight.

Refusing to acknowledge the feelings of defeat, Shay ran towards the narrow end of the gap as fast as she could. But just like in a dream, it kept moving further and further away, as if permanently out of reach. After running for a solid half hour, she stopped as tears began fall. There was no way she'd finish her trial in time. She was never going to get her wings or become a full-fledge fairy, and never was she going to be Queen, as her vision had implied.

Shay sank to her knees and wept into her hands, but suddenly lifted her head when she heard a strange sound. It was the same sound that had woken her from her slumber on the banks of the Lake of Sorrow. A high whistle that she didn't recognize belonging to any animal she could think of. But as she opened her eyes she saw the silver strands of her hair glowing brightly, she was grateful for whatever or whoever it was that had gained her attention. She had already received so much help from the fairy spirits, and it seemed as if they were preparing to help her once more. Smiling, Shay closed her eyes and opened her mind to let the words of the divine spirits flow into her again.

Shay quickly searched her travel bag and retrieved the spell bottle. Uncorking it, she quickly drank the potion then chanted,

"Lord of the sun, Queen of the moon, hear me know as I ask for a boon. Lengthen my day, only when needed. Focus my will when patience's depleted. Magick forged by moon and sun, as I say it, so will it be done."

Shay opened her eyes to find the moon repositioned by almost two hours. By magick, it was again 10 p.m. She jumped to her feet and thanked the spirits as she started on her journey once more.

Shay walked patiently this time, constantly keeping her eye on the exactly place where she wanted to cross. Within twenty minutes she stood at the edge of the gap where it was thin enough to jump across.

Easily making it to the other side, she looked back only to see the entire chasm completely disappear. Smiling and shaking her head at the same time, she began her trek to the castle again.

Reaching it within ten minutes, Shay gathered her thoughts, smoothed her hair, and straightened her clothes before knocking on the massive wood door. She stared at the intricate carved detail as she waited for a response. There were fairies and their treetop homes carved with such amazing precision they could've easily been copied from a live example. The Rune Tree was featured as well, and the final detail Shay noticed before the door swung open was a small box, with ribbons cascading down its sides in the center of the door. The Box of Nye.

Taking in the massive entrance, Shay slowly entered the Queen's castle. There was no one there to greet her, as the door had apparently opened on its own. Noting the time before entering, Shay had an hour and a half to find the box and complete her trial. And according to the runes, the next thing she needed to find was the love that had been lost.

Walking down the corridor that veered to the right, Shay quickly found the chambers of the fey council. She knew that Joseph was the person she needed to find. She wondered if he knew his part in all of this when he'd come to her house this morning, or if he was just as clueless about their intertwined future as she had been.

Entering the chamber she found Joe sitting alone at the long wooden table.

"You made it," he said.

Apparently he did have a clue. Shay giggled and remembered his wink as he left her house just this morning.

"Yes. I made it. Question is...why exactly am I here? What do you have to do with my trial and the box?"

"Shay, I'm sure you've noticed that your hair has not only started to develop it's magickal colors, but that you've already been able to use your magick even though you aren't a full-fledge fairy yet."

"Yes. The fairy spirits have been very kind in aiding me," Shay replied.

"They aid you like they've never aided anyone before...anyone except the Queen." Joe stood and walked towards Shay. Kneeling in front of her, he took her hand in his as he continued, "Shay, you are destined to become our next Queen, and I am to be your Hand."

The Queen's Hand was someone who not only guided and aided her in all things related to fairy business, but was also the love of her life. The Hand was chosen by the fairy spirits, just as the Queen was, and also carried silver magick. Shay looked down at Joe and noticed the silver strands that had added themselves to his red ones.

"This morning, after seeing you again after all these years, I felt the love I had for you back then reignite in my chest. In was in that instant that silver streaks began to weave their way through my hair. The other council members were surprised but happy and explained the new destiny that was in store for us both. Shay, I'm not sure how you feel, but I want you to know that I'm so proud and happy to be your Hand. I've missed you."

Shay pulled Joe from his knee and flung herself into his arms. "I've missed you too and I couldn't be happier."

Their embrace quickly escalated to a kiss and Shay knew they were truly a perfect match for one another. The idea of building a life with Joe excited her beyond words, but there was still the fact that she needed to complete her trial or none of this "new destiny" would even matter.

"Joe, I have to go and complete my trial. I still haven't found the final item and I'm running out of time. I'll be back as soon as I can."

Joe's smile lit up his handsome face, and with a wink he said, "Farewell, my lady, I'll be waiting for your return. Oh, and Shay...make sure you shut the door on your way out."

Shay laughed and gave a little wave as she ran back towards the massive front door of the castle. Just as she grabbed the handle and pulled, the silver strands in her hair started tingling again. Stepping outside she didn't look back as she pushed the door close with a shove from behind. The door however, wouldn't budge. Shay continued to stare out into the night as she pushed behind her again, this time with a little more force. Still, the door didn't move.

Turning around to actually face the massive door, Shay pushed again. It moved only a fraction which left Shay confused and frustrated. Placing both hands on the door, she dug in her heels and really started to shove. It finally began to close, but the task was not easy. By the time it was back in place, her face was practically plastered into the wood carvings. And just as she started to pull away something caught her eye.

Just above the iron handle was a carving in the shape of a key. She hadn't noticed it before but now it was all she could see. With her attention fully focused on the door, Shay found multiple key images throughout its intricate design. She smiled as her hair began to tingling wildly, and she knew she was about to find the final item of her trial.

Cursing herself for not remembering sooner, Shay now recalled stories her mother had told her when she was a little girl. When the first fairy Queen was chosen by the spirits, they gifted her with a beautiful castle that included an enchanted wooden door made from the Rune Tree itself.

Shay quickly scanned the entire structure and found all the key images. They were all in the shape of an antique skeleton-type key, with a fairy star that rested on top. Each was a different size and positioned in odd places, but only one stood out to Shay. It was the one carved to look like it was lying in the grass right next to the Rune Tree.

Shay gently ran her fingertip across the raised relief of the key. Nothing happened. She did it again and again, but always with the same result. The key didn't budge or do anything magickal at all. Panicking she had the wrong image Shay started running her fingers over all the keys as fast as she could. None of them moved. She thought about how hard she'd worked to get to this moment and recapped everything she'd done: fought the animals in the Feygan forest to retrieve the trig owl's feather; shook off the eerie depression from the Lake of Sorrow and embraced her water magic to retrieve the rasper shell; and received a vision at the Rune Tree that led her here and to her lost love.

Joe! she thought, snapping her head up. She recalled the last words he had just said to her. *"...make sure you shut the door on your way out."* A door she had to push...hard. Shay immediately raised her fingers back to the first key and this time instead of lightly touching it she gave it a hard push.

The key immediately released and flew from the carving, landing directly in her hand. "Yes!" she cried. As she turned around, the portal appeared before her and she stepped through, knowing she was only moments away from finding the Box of Nye.

Shay found herself back in the ancient forest of the Rune Tree. It was only fifteen minutes until midnight so she started running, desperate to begin her search. Suddenly, moonlight broke through the tall trees to illuminate a beautiful white box with sparkling silver ribbons tied in a bow, its ends flowing down the sides, resting immediately in her path. It was picture perfect. Snow glistened and the box shimmered in the beam of moonlight that shot straight down from heaven.

Shay raced to the box then fell on her knees in the snow. Reaching out, she gently untied the bow and lifted the lid. The white light that erupted from the box was warm and encompassing. Though she had to close her eyes against the brightness, Shay could feel herself being lifted into the air as the light wrapped around her like a cocoon. Her back began to tingle as her wings started to emerge, and a colorful glow radiated around her as more blue and silver streaks wound themselves throughout her hair.

Moments later, Shay drifted gently back to earth, her trial over, and her transformation into a full-fledged fairy complete. She turned to see the boxed had disappeared and the portal was once again shimmering, waiting for her to enter.

Shay put her new glittering wings to use and flew straight towards the portal. She emerged back at the castle to find Joe, the other two council members, and the Queen, waiting for her outside the front door.

"Congratulations, Shay. You have not only completed your fairy trial, but have taken the first step in one day becoming my replacement," the Queen said.

Shay bowed and smiled before speaking. "Thank you, my Queen. Though I doubt I will ever be as great a Queen as you."

The Queen laughed and it sounded like bells tinkling on the wind. She then walked forward and hugged Shay in a kind embrace. "My dear, Shay. You were born to be my replacement and your love, Joseph, was born to be your Hand. However, it will be many years before you'll be called to duty, so I now send you home to enjoy Christmas with your family and to start building your new life together."

"Thank you, my Queen," Shay replied. She then held out her hand to Joseph, and was overwhelmed with excitement as they walked through the portal together, emerging back at her family's home.

Suddenly Shay turned to Joe. "Wait. I remember everything...how can that be? I thought all memories of my trial were to be wiped from my mind."

"Yes, that is usually what happens for all fairies...except the Queen. You're special Shay, you always have been." Joseph kissed her lightly and walked towards the house, smiling wide because he knew, on this Christmas morning there was one more surprise Shay would be experiencing.

Narine tightly hugged both Shay and Joe when they entered the kitchen. "Shay, I'm so proud of you. My daughter...the soon to be Queen."

"How did you know, Mama?"

"I didn't. Not until the council members came back after you left and informed me of the situation. They explained that you were meant to be the Queen's replacement one day, and that Joseph here was your chosen Hand. They also left you this." She gestured to a small box under the Christmas tree. It was a tiny replica of the Box of Nye.

Shay rushed to open it and found a miniature key and a note inside. "Dear Shay and Joseph. Please accept this gift from me. Use this key and begin your journey together with my blessing." It was signed, "Queen Raeanne."

Suddenly another portal opened up right in the middle of the small kitchen, Joe and Shay stepped through, followed by Narine and the rest of Shay's family. The pure shock and overwhelming joy they were all sharing was the best Christmas present Shay ever had.

The Queen had gifted Shay and Joseph a new house. It

was a smaller version of the Queen's castle and sat atop the hill that overlooked Shay's village. Joe scooped Shay into his arms and flew up into the sky, spinning them both around and around. "Merry Christmas, future Queen. I love you so much. Now let's go home."

THE END

Look for Shay and her fairies throughout the Ovialell series.

BONUS MATERIAL

SAMHAIN IN OVALELL

by

Tish Thawer

(A behind the scenes look from Aradia Awakens)

Tonight wasn't a celebration of All Hallows Eve, or Halloween. You wouldn't see any children dressed up in silly costumes, racing from door to door gathering candy from their neighbors. Not here. Not in Ovialell.

Instead, on this Samhain night, there was going to be a grand ceremony to welcome back the Queen of The Witches.

The Witches were a coven of powerful witches who run with the Goddess Diana during the wild hunt, and are charged with protecting us citizens of Ovialell with their magick and healing abilities.

When the Goddess Diana sent out word that the Queen had returned, an elaborate event had been planned to welcome her back. Now, I won't pretend that we aren't all skeptical, I mean, it's common knowledge that the Queen had been killed during the Great Rift. But if the Goddess says she's back—combined with the fact that Queen Shay, the leader of the Seelie Fae, had already arrived; not to mention Kylie and her Amazon warriors were expected any minute—yeah...this was exciting stuff. Everyone in Ovialell would be attending *this* ceremony to see exactly who this "Queen" really was.

My name is Lexxi, and my mom use to be one of The Witches. Her name was Ingrid, but she was killed about six months ago. After that the Goddess allowed me to live and work in her castle on Upper World; that's how I was able to get a sneak peek at the throne room where the ceremony would be held tonight.

The lavish decorations had my jaw dropping the first time I'd snuck in the side entrance from the kitchen. The velvet curtains surrounding the raised dais where the Goddess would introduce the new Queen from, looked so heavy that it would probably take a spell to actually move them. There was a red carpet runner that flowed down the middle of the room, separating it into two distinct sections. It was so long it looked like a river of blood against the white marble floor.

There were fairy lights throughout the room, courtesy of the Fae, I'm sure. They floated in the air of their own accord and twinkled with a hue that wasn't found anywhere on Upper World. Since the Fae— Seelie and Unseelie—both resided on the Middle World of Ovialell, the fact that they were here was a pretty big deal.

I was so ready for this ceremony to get started. I'd dressed hours ago, then came to help out in any way that I could. My dress wasn't too fancy, but I thought it was pretty. The long navy skirt was velvet and there was fine gold piping that was braided to look like a net which laid atop the whole thing. The bodice was gold and the undershirt the same navy blue as the skirt. My friend had pulled the laces so tight that my cleavage was ridiculously exaggerated. I'd decided to leave my hair down, but wound in some little braids to match my dress. I thought my blonde hair went well with the blue and gold.

It was almost time for the ceremony to begin and I hoped that I could maintain a good position to see everything. So, as everyone started to enter the throne room, I staked out a place behind one of the stone pillars. I figured I could use it's tiered bottom to stand on in order to get an extra boost to see over the crowd. But just as the door shut, some rude red-haired woman nudged me off of my spot. When I turned to state that I'd been there first, I found myself staring into a pair reddish-brown eyes, which ironically, were the last thing I'd ever see. Because when she opened her mouth to smile, all I saw were a set of fangs.

Other books by Tish Thawer:

The Ovialell Series:

Aradia Awakens - Book 1

(Available Now)

The Rose Trilogy:

Scent of a White Rose - Book 1

(Available Now)

Roses & Thorns - Book 1.5

(Available Now)

Blood of a Red Rose - Book 2

(Available Now)

Death of a Black Rose - Book 3

(Available 2013)